M000074392

Oblivion

Carly Mensch

A SAMUEL FRENCH ACTING EDITION

SAMUEL
FRENCH
FOUNDED 1830

SAMUELFRENCH.COM
SAMUELFRENCH-LONDON.CO.UK

Copyright © 2015 by Carly Mensch
All Rights Reserved

OBLIVION is fully protected under the copyright laws of the United States
of America, the British Commonwealth, including Canada, and all other
countries of the Copyright Union. All rights, including professional and
amateur stage productions, recitation, lecturing, public reading, motion
picture, radio broadcasting, television and the rights of translation into
foreign languages are strictly reserved.

ISBN 978-0-573-70366-9

www.SamuelFrench.com
www.SamuelFrench-London.co.uk

FOR PRODUCTION ENQUIRIES

UNITED STATES AND CANADA
Info@SamuelFrench.com
1-866-598-8449

UNITED KINGDOM AND EUROPE
Plays@SamuelFrench-London.co.uk
020-7255-4302

Each title is subject to availability from Samuel French, depending upon
country of performance. Please be aware that *OBLIVION* may not be
licensed by Samuel French in your territory. Professional and amateur
producers should contact the nearest Samuel French office or licensing
partner to verify availability.

CAUTION: Professional and amateur producers are hereby warned that
OBLIVION is subject to a licensing fee. Publication of this play(s) does
not imply availability for performance. Both amateurs and professionals
considering a production are strongly advised to apply to Samuel French
before starting rehearsals, advertising, or booking a theatre. A licensing
fee must be paid whether the title(s) is presented for charity or gain and
whether or not admission is charged. Professional/Stock licensing fees
are quoted upon application to Samuel French.

No one shall make any changes in this title(s) for the purpose of
production. No part of this book may be reproduced, stored in a retrieval
system, or transmitted in any form, by any means, now known or yet to
be invented, including mechanical, electronic, photocopying, recording,
videotaping, or otherwise, without the prior written permission of the
publisher. No one shall upload this title(s), or part of this title(s), to any
social media websites.

For all enquiries regarding motion picture, television, and other media
rights, please contact Samuel French.

MUSIC USE NOTE

Licensees are solely responsible for obtaining formal written permission from copyright owners to use copyrighted music in the performance of this play and are strongly cautioned to do so. If no such permission is obtained by the licensee, then the licensee must use only original music that the licensee owns and controls. Licensees are solely responsible and liable for all music clearances and shall indemnify the copyright owners of the play(s) and their licensing agent, Samuel French, against any costs, expenses, losses and liabilities arising from the use of music by licensees. Please contact the appropriate music licensing authority in your territory for the rights to any incidental music.

IMPORTANT BILLING AND CREDIT REQUIREMENTS

If you have obtained performance rights to this title, please refer to your licensing agreement for important billing and credit requirements.

OBLIVION was first produced by the Westport Country Playhouse (Mark Lamos, Artistic Director; Michael Ross, Managing Director) in Westport, Connecticut. The opening night was August 24, 2013. The performance was directed by Mark Brokaw, with sets by Neil Patel, costumes by Michael Krass, lighting by Japhy Weideman, and sound/original music by Obadiah Evans. The Production Stage Manager was Matthew Melchiorre. The cast was as follows:

PAM	Johanna Day
DIXON	Reg Rogers
JULIE	Katie Broad
BERNARD	Aidan Kunze

OBLIVION was developed by Steppenwolf Theatre Company through its New Plays Initiative and was presented as part of its First Look Repertory of New Work at Steppenwolf Theatre Company, Chicago, Illinois (Martha Lavey, Artistic Director; David Hawkanson, Executive Director).

OBLIVION was commissioned by Playwrights Horizons with funds provided by Kate and Seymour Weingarten

CHARACTERS

PAM – 40's
DIXON – 40's
JULIE – 16
BERNARD – 16

SETTING

Brooklyn, New York

TIME

Now

ACT ONE

1.

(A sprawling loft apartment. Exposed brick, books everywhere.)

(JULIE, a lanky girl in basketball sweats, sits in the hot seat being interrogated by her mother, PAM. Her father, DIXON, meanwhile, a big, artfully disheveled guy, sits nearby reading The New Yorker.)

(We are hours into this fight and everyone's feeling it. Stalemate.)

PAM. Just say it. Just say it and we can all go to bed.

JULIE. Say what?

PAM. How many hours are you going to keep this up for?

JULIE. I'm telling the truth.

PAM. You are not.

JULIE. I am.

PAM. Jules. I'm tired. Your Dad's tired. Everyone's tired.

(JULIE shrugs.)

Dixon, can you please say something here?

(beat)

DIXON. Don't lie. Lying is bad.

(DIXON goes back to reading.)

PAM. Dix!

DIXON. What?

PAM. Don't make me the bad guy here.

DIXON. I'm not. I said don't lie. She shouldn't lie, right? I said that.

JULIE. Is this because of menopause?

PAM. Excuse me?

JULIE. You're being like, really irrational.

PAM. I am way, *way* too young for that, thank you very much.

JULIE. You're 46.

PAM. Okay. I see what you're doing here. Not going to work.

JULIE. I'm just stating the facts. You're 46. That's how old you are.

(**DIXON** *smirks.* **JULIE** *notices and smirks too.* **PAM** *notices both of them. They stop.*)

(**PAM** *holds up a glossy Wesleyan brochure.*)

PAM. Tell me about Wesleyan.

JULIE. Again?

PAM. Yes.

JULIE. I've told you like three times.

PAM. You arrived Saturday morning.

JULIE. Yeah. We took Metro North, Saturday morning, like I told you.

PAM. And then – Bernard's sister picked you up.

JULIE. Uh huh.

PAM. Can I have her number?

JULIE. I don't have it.

PAM. You spent the entire weekend with her yet you didn't write down her cell phone number?

JULIE. Yeah, because Bernard had it.

PAM. What about classes? What classes did you sit in on?

JULIE. Intro to French Lit.

PAM. What was the topic?

JULIE. Roland Barthes.

PAM. The same Roland Barthes you're currently learning about in *high school* French class?

JULIE. Yeah.

PAM. Hmm. What a coincidence.

JULIE. He's a popular twentieth century figure.

PAM. So they have classes on weekends? At Wesleyan?

JULIE. … No. It was a study group. Sorry. But the TA was there. Because, the prof had cancelled a class earlier that week. So it was like a make-up class.

(*beat*)

PAM. Ladies and Gentleman. I rest my case!

JULIE. No!

PAM. Julie – if you didn't go to Wesleyan, I don't care. Just tell me. I will not be offended if you don't want to go to my alma mater. Even though, it's a very good school. You should consider it.

JULIE. I did. I went.

PAM. Clearly you didn't.

JULIE. *Clearly* you're acting like a psychotic bitch.

(*pause*)

(**DIXON** *sees* **PAM**'s *hurt.*)

DIXON. This writer. He keeps using this construction "and yet but so." *And yet but so.* I don't even know what that means. It's like some Boolean logic problem. Like he translated the whole thing into Russian, took out all the verbs and then translated it back into English. This is the goddamn New Yorker for chrissake. It's called *standards* of American English. It's called basic human decency.

PAM. (*softly*) Honey.

DIXON. What?

PAM. You're performing.

DIXON. I was just trying –
Nevermind.

(silence)

PAM. Julie. Your integrity is vital. If your dad and I can teach you one thing – instill one fundamental moral value – it's to always, always tell the truth.

(pause)

JULIE. *Always?*

PAM. Yes. Always.

JULIE. But. You're a moral relativist.

PAM. … So?

JULIE. You and Dad. You don't believe in right and wrong.

PAM. Okay. That is a *gross* misinterpretation of moral relativism.

JULIE. That's what it sounds like.

PAM. What what sounds like?

JULIE. Your…belief system.

PAM. You think our belief system amounts to "Do whatever you want?"

JULIE. … No. I'm just saying.

PAM. Yes. Please explain to me your logic this evening. Please.

JULIE. I don't know! Okay? I just don't understand why this is such a big deal. It's like you guys suddenly turned into the Gestapo. You gave me permission to go away this weekend, I went, I came back, and so. What's the big deal?

PAM. The big deal is you *lied* to us.

JULIE. I didn't!

PAM. I give up.

(to **DIXON***)* Can you please explain to her why she's wrong? She listens to you.

(DIXON *lowers the magazine.)*

DIXON. Julie – you're lying. We already know that. It's a white lie, so, whatever, fuck it, doesn't really matter. We don't actually care wherever you happened to be gallivanting around this weekend since you're clearly still alive and breathing. But we *do* care about the fact you seem to be so *nonchalant* about lying to us, especially since we're pretty chilled out people who are trying to impart some actual *knowledge* to you – mainly, if you want to have a rich and meaningful *relationship* with someone, in this case, us, you should bite the bullet, swallow your pride and learn to tell the truth. This isn't some pre-packaged dogma bullshit we're trying to brainwash you with here. This is about basic human trust. Like real basic human being shit. Also, this is clearly driving your mom insane. So. Think of the larger picture.

(beat)

PAM. Do you have anything you want to say to us now?

(**JULIE** *thinks about it.*)

JULIE. No.

2.

*(The laundromat. **JULIE** and **BERNARD** wait for clothes to finish in the dryer. **BERNARD**, a nerdy Korean kid aims an old-school Super-8 camera at **JULIE**'s face.)*

BERNARD. Can you look away, like, wistful?

JULIE. Why am I wistful?

BERNARD. It doesn't matter.

*(**JULIE** looks away wistfully while **BERNARD** films.)*

JULIE. Can you *believe* I have to wash my own clothes? It's like I'm homeless.

BERNARD. Aren't you guys rich? Don't you have like people doing your laundry in the basement?

JULIE. I'm being punished for calling my Mom a psychotic bitch. I hate my mom.

BERNARD. Your Mom is awesome.

JULIE. Trust me. She's like, a monster. You would be totally terrified of her.

BERNARD. She works for HBO. She's like – my hero.

JULIE. She sits behind a desk. She's not like – an artist or anything.

BERNARD. Wait! Don't move.

JULIE. Why not?

BERNARD. Just stay exactly as you are right now.

*(**BERNARD** rubs some chapstick on the camera lens then films the perfect shot of **JULIE**.)*

JULIE. Can I move yet?

BERNARD. No.

JULIE. Does your film have a story or is it just me doing random things?

BERNARD. You're my protagonist.

JULIE. But I never really do anything.

BERNARD. It's a generational portrait.

JULIE. Did you get the three-pointer I made against Fieldston?

BERNARD. Yeah.

JULIE. I want a copy of that.

BERNARD. Okay.

JULIE. What are you going to do with it when you're finished?

BERNARD. Send it to Pauline Kael.

JULIE. Who's Pauline Kael?

BERNARD. *You* don't know who Pauline Kael is?

JULIE. No.

BERNARD. How can you live in New York City and not know who Pauline Kael is?

(**BERNARD** *turns off the camera. He goes to his backpack and pulls out an old battered copy of Pauline Kael's For Keeps. It's a massive tome, over 1,000 pages.*)

It's basically my bible.

JULIE. So who is she?

BERNARD. A film critic. A really, really important film critic.

JULIE. Oh.

BERNARD. I've read this book maybe five hundred times. I have the preface memorized.

JULIE. So what. You're just going to send it to her?

BERNARD. That's what Wes Anderson did with his first film. He just drove to her house in Massachusetts and made her watch it. I heard him say that on Charlie Rose.

JULIE. What if she doesn't like it?

BERNARD. She probably won't. She doesn't really like anything.

JULIE. So then why are you sending it to her?

BERNARD. I need brutal honesty, not the blind encouragement of my peers.

(**JULIE** *checks on her clothes to see if they're done.*)

JULIE. My Mom. She's totally spazzing out about last weekend. Just, FYI.

BERNARD. Why? What did you tell her?

JULIE. I said I was with you.

BERNARD. So why is she spazzing out?

JULIE. Because I also said we went to Wesleyan and hung out with your sister and a bunch of other minor details.

(*beat*)

BERNARD. I don't have a sister.

JULIE. Who's that girl who's always at your house?

BERNARD. Sue-Jean? My cousin?

JULIE. Crap!

BERNARD. I'm an only child. That's why I'm so independent and non-competitive.

JULIE. Do you think if my parents called Sue-Jean, she could say she's your sister?

BERNARD. You're parents want to call my cousin!?

JULIE. No. Just if for some reason –

BERNARD. I knew it! I knew this was a bad idea.

JULIE. They're not gonna do it.

BERNARD. I don't understand why you can't just tell them.

JULIE. My parents?

BERNARD. Yes. They're like, the most open-minded liberal people on the planet.

JULIE. They are not open-minded.

BERNARD. Uh huh.

JULIE. You've never even met them. They think they're so above everyone.

BERNARD. Whatever. My parents never even went to college. If they find out I entangled my cousin in some white kid's cover-up story, I'm gonna be like sent to like, North Korea.

JULIE. My parents aren't going to entangle anyone. Because then they would have to pretend they actually care

where I was, which they don't. My Dad even admitted
it. He said they're just trying to teach me a lesson
about "ethics" or something.

BERNARD. I hate lying.

JULIE. You don't have to *lie;* just don't say anything.

BERNARD. I'm not like you. I can't just make stuff up on
the spot.

JULIE. They're not gonna ask.

BERNARD. Good.

JULIE. But…if for some reason…

BERNARD. See! I knew it!

JULIE. Just if they ask.

All you have to do is confirm we went on a college tour.
Which is half-true since we slept in a dorm.

Come on. How many hours have I put into this movie?
I'm your protagonist, Bernard. You need me. Your film
needs me.

Like, if for some reason I was to drop out –

BERNARD. No!

JULIE. Promise then?

(**BERNARD** *looks at* **JULIE**. *He adores her.*)

BERNARD. … Fine.

JULIE. Say it: I promise.

BERNARD. I promise.

3.

(Later that evening. Game night. **PAM** *and* **DIXON** *laze picnic-style on the floor. It's been a good night – a.k.a. whisky and Boggle. Nearby, a plastic hourglass counts down as they scribble words on little notepads.)*

PAM. Hey! Oh my god you are so cheating.

DIXON. I was just comparing.

PAM. How come there are so many vowels? Are you only seeing vowels?

DIXON. Look clockwise.

PAM. Where? I think I'm –

DIXON. Cognitively compromised? Agreed.

PAM. I'm not!

DIXON. You're a lightweight. That was part of my strategy.

PAM. You got me *drunk?*

DIXON. I got us both drunk – level playing field.

(They play.)

PAM. Do you think Julie drinks?

DIXON. She might be drinking protein powder. The occasional energy drink.

PAM. She should.

DIXON. Drink?

PAM. Yeah. She might loosen up a bit. She's so…

DIXON. You're saying, you want our kid to be a lush?

PAM. Not a lush! But a recreational drinker would be fine. I wish she went out more. You know? To parties. Had more friends.

DIXON. She's got Bernard.

PAM. Bernard is a God-send. He's a saint. He's a –

DIXON. Time!

PAM. What? Already?

DIXON. Yeah, we forgot about the timer.

*(**DIXON** scribbles one last word.)*

PAM. Hey!

(They swap answer pads to tabulate scores.)

DIXON. *(looking at* **PAM** *'s words)* Yup. Had that. Had that.

PAM. *(looking at* **DIXON** *'s)* SLURPY?

DIXON. Not bad, right?

PAM. SLURPY is not a word.

DIXON. It's a noun.

PAM. It's a beverage.

DIXON. It's a genre of beverage.

PAM. I'll give you two points for SLURP.

DIXON. Three. It's a meaningful utterance.

PAM. …. You take one linguistics class in college and…

DIXON. I am a word connoisseur. Yup. Three points please.

PAM. No way, and I will use brute force if I have to.

*(***PAM** *makes a grab for his answer pad.)*

DIXON. You're very adorable when you drink. You get all self-righteous.

PAM. Because you're a bully.

DIXON. *Two points.* No points.

PAM. Games have rules. That's like, the defining element of a game.

DIXON. See what I mean? Don't worry, it's cute.

PAM. Hey – condescending.

DIXON. Forgive me, you're a strong, independent woman.

PAM. Thank you.

DIXON. You're Madame Vice President.

PAM. Madame *Senior* Vice President.

DIXON. ….freakin' Rosie the Riveter.

DIXON. Come here.

(They kiss.)

*(***PAM** *pulls away suddenly.)*

PAM. Am I a bitch?

DIXON. In general…?

PAM. You didn't say anything. When Julie called me that.

DIXON. I…apologize. I was playing Switzerland.

PAM. She's never behaved like this before. Lied to us? To our faces?

DIXON. Well. Not that we know of.

PAM. She used to tell us everything. When that creep Elliot Crumbine offered her ecstasy. She woke me up in the middle of the night to talk about it. Now. It's like I'm the enemy.

DIXON. Mother daughter stuff is tricky.

PAM. Do we punish her? Is that how we're supposed to deal with this?

DIXON. Off with her head!

PAM. Because she has to learn. We are not okay with this.

DIXON. No…

PAM. …And it's not just something you learn intellectually. You have to *feel* it. It's something you have to learn with your whole body.

DIXON. Mm-hmm. Body. Yes.

PAM. Before it's programmed in. You know? Before it becomes a habit.

DIXON. Before what becomes a habit?

PAM. Lying.

DIXON. Oh. We're still on that?

PAM. You don't think it's important?

DIXON. What?

PAM. Integrity.

DIXON. Sure, in theory.

PAM. In life.

DIXON. We should play more Boggle. Boggle is a fun game.

PAM. You never take me seriously.

DIXON. I never take anything seriously.

PAM. I'm trying to say something here.

DIXON. You want me to break out the philosophy books? Have a real debate with you? Cause I can do that –

PAM. Okay.

DIXON. Okay well I'm not going to do that. You'd demolish me.

PAM. I think we fucked up somewhere. Parenting wise.

DIXON. We did not fuck up.

PAM. Somehow we've given her the impression that we have no moral standards, so clearly she's in need of *some* parameters.

DIXON. I thought we decided never to be like this. Parents with rules.

PAM. She lied to us. To our faces.

DIXON. C'mon. You lie. I lie. Everybody lies.

PAM. I do not lie.

DIXON. You've definitely lied to me.

PAM. I never lie to you.

DIXON. Not like Machiavellian deception…

PAM. No. Never.

DIXON. Okay. You probably don't even notice it.

PAM. Try me.

DIXON. Okay. Fine. Do you like this shirt?

PAM. *(honestly)* No.

DIXON. Do you think it's good I quit my job?

PAM. Definitely.

DIXON. Really?

PAM. It was killing you. Plus. Corporate law is evil and depressing and now you have the opportunity to expose those craven ass-holes in a tell-all best-selling book.

DIXON. I love you. That's the truth. No room for argument there. Kiss me again.

(**PAM** *hesitates, but does and soon relaxes into him again. Paradise restored.*)

PAM. Read to me from your book.

DIXON. And kill the mood?

PAM. I like being proud of you.

DIXON. Well in that case…

> (**DIXON** *gets his laptop.*)

PAM. We should send it to John Grisham. We should track down John Grisham and send it to him.

DIXON. Actually – he went to law school with one of our former associates.

> (*He opens it open. Clicks open a document.*)

> (*He lets her read over his shoulder.*)

Do you need context?

PAM. No. I remember. The guy sued the other guy and some judge is in jail.

DIXON. Close enough.

> (*reading*) "First case is Schneiter versus Magruder," Spicer announced as if a major antitrust trial was about to start.

> "Schneiter's not here," Beech said."
> "Where is he?"
> "Infirmary. Gallstones again."

PAM. Gallstones!

DIXON. "… Beach was fifty-six, the youngest of the three, and with nine years to go he was convinced he would die in prison. He'd been a federal judge in East Texas, a hardfisted conservative who knew lots of Scripture and liked to quote it during trials."

That's enough for tonight.

PAM. No! I love it. I love gallstones.

DIXON. It still needs work.

PAM. It's great. I think it's so brave what you're doing. Starting over. I couldn't do it.

> (**PAM** *smiles.*)

PAM. We should smoke.

DIXON. *(feigning)* What!?

PAM. I know you have some.

DIXON. I might have some left over. Maybe.

> *(beat)*

> I am very surprised you're initiating this. Wait. Unless this is a trap?

PAM. We're adults.

DIXON. I thought you didn't like me smoking.

PAM. I don't like you smoking alone. With me is fine.

DIXON. All these rules of yours… It's very hard to keep track.

> **(JULIE** *enters carrying her backpack and sport bag. She stares at them on the floor. Disturbed, disapproving.)*

PAM. Want to come join us? We're having a very romantic game night.

> *(beat)*

DIXON. Boggle.

> **(JULIE** *stares at them some more.)*

JULIE. Practice went late. Call coach if you don't believe me.

4.

(The next day. **DIXON** *is home alone. He wears a bathrobe and pajama pants and has a work-station set up that consists of a laptop and some library books. He's not working, however. He's rolling a joint. A box of Nilla wafers sits nearby.)*

(After a moment, the sound of someone at the front door. Keys jangling. **DIXON** *hides the joint. Enter* **BERNARD**.*)*

BERNARD. Julie said you wouldn't be home.

DIXON. Of course I'm home. I work from home.

BERNARD. *(avoiding eye contact)* Don't you have, um, a shift at the Food Co-op?

DIXON. Shit. Is it Thursday?

BERNARD. Yeah.

DIXON. Guess we're not having organic brussels sprouts for dinner.

Do you know that place? In Park Slope. It's a very passive-aggressive grocery store.

BERNARD. No. I live in Queens. We shop at this place H-Mart.

(beat)

I'm Bernard.

DIXON. I figured.

(pause)

BERNARD. I should go.

DIXON. No, I've been hoping to meet you for a while. So, this is actually quite serendipitous. Stay. Chillax.

*(***BERNARD** *doesn't chillax.)*

BERNARD. Julie forgot to bring in the poster for our French presentation.

DIXON. On what?

BERNARD. Carla Bruni. The supermodel turned pop singer turned political trophy wife.

DIXON. Only in France, right?

BERNARD. Only in France what?

DIXON. A sex symbol as first lady. Part of my book is set in France. In the South. It's very sensual. Very French.

BERNARD. You're writing a book?

DIXON. Yup. First time.

BERNARD. I thought you were a lawyer.

DIXON. Was. The law was starting to feel a little too stringent. I'm much more interested in grey areas now. And I had a little... I guess what you'd call a minor breakdown. I'm sure Julie told you...?

BERNARD. Yeah.

(*beat*)

I'm making a film.

DIXON. Oh yeah?

BERNARD. It's black and white. Silent.

DIXON. Sounds like a real block-buster.

BERNARD. It's a generational portrait.

DIXON. You dress very strangely.

BERNARD. Thanks.

(*pause*)

Julie has class.

DIXON. I told you. Water under the bridge.

BERNARD. I had a free so I said I'd come. I'm just trying to explain why I interrupted –

DIXON. You're not interrupting.

BERNARD. Cause it looked like I was interrupting...

(**BERNARD** *timidly nods to the joint.*)

DIXON. Ah. Busted.

(*beat*)

You want in?

BERNARD. Is that –

DIXON. Pot? Yes. I'm not condoning it. Just offering.

BERNARD. Uh –

DIXON. No pressure. Totally your decision.

BERNARD. Okay.

DIXON. Okay you want some?

BERNARD. … Sure.

DIXON. Don't tell Pam though. She doesn't like when I smoke during the day.

BERNARD. Is Pam…?

DIXON. My wife.

BERNARD. Right. I only know your last names.

DIXON. Back in the spring, I was up to about a gram, gram and a half a day. Self-medicating, filling the void, that sort of thing. Now that I quit my job though, I'm much more of a recreational abuser.

(**DIXON** *lights the joint and passes it to* **BERNARD**. *They pass back and forth during the following conversation.*)

Can I ask you something personal?

BERNARD. …Um. Okay.

DIXON. Would you mind listening to some of my book?

BERNARD. *(relieved)* Yeah. Sure. I thought you were…. Nevermind.

DIXON. I haven't shared this with anybody yet. But. Since you're a fellow artist. And well, frankly, I could use a man's perspective.

It's on the laptop.

BERNARD. Oh.

(**DIXON** *gestures to the laptop.* **BERNARD** *retrieves it.*)

DIXON. Seriously though. This is top secret stuff.

This chapter is called. The French Ambassador's Daughter.

(reading) "… He leaned her back against the desk, back against the splintering sunlit mahogany. Her hair knotted up in one of those awe-inspiring messy buns she liked to wear. She was

awe-inspiring, the French Ambassador's daughter. She was also epileptic, which accounted for the ad hoc seizures she often drifted in and out of during sex. She gripped the desk behind her. His mouth dropped open, his very core pulsating with the *stuff* of the earth. He leaned in and whispered into her ear: "Have you taken your medication?" "No," she replied. "But I like it better this way."

(beat)

So?

BERNARD. You wrote that?

DIXON. Yes. Yes, I did.

BERNARD. It's good. It's cinematic. Like I could see it in a movie.

DIXON. You're a smart kid Bernard.

You know, you kids are lucky, growing up in the city.

The access to culture. The constant stimuli.

I can already see the effect on Julie. She's much more resourceful than I was at that age. Tougher too.

BERNARD. Well, she is a Varsity athlete.

DIXON. Right? How twisted is that: Two urban sophisticates give birth to a high school basketball player. Go figure. What about you. You play any sports?

BERNARD. No. I'm non-competitive, in general.

DIXON. I hear that. I hear ya.

(beat)

I have an enlarged prostate.

BERNARD. Excuse me?

DIXON. Just doing the guy talk here. Trying to loosen the mood.

BERNARD. I'm sorry.

DIXON. Hey. No pity. You live, you die, right? Can't do anything about it.

BERNARD. I guess not.

DIXON. Let me ask you something Bernard.

You and Julie. You two've been spending a lot of time together.

BERNARD. Yeah.

DIXON. Julie doesn't have many other friends, I've noticed.

BERNARD. She has her teammates, but. I guess she's not really close to any of them.

DIXON. So you'd say you're pretty intimate.

BERNARD. We're not –

DIXON. I'm not asking about that.

BERNARD. Oh. So what are you asking?

DIXON. This last weekend. Just between you and me. You don't have to give me details.

(**BERNARD** *freezes.*)

I just want to make sure Julie's not in over her head.

BERNARD. Trust me, she's not.

DIXON. I'm just looking for a general sense, that's all.

BERNARD. Really. It's nothing serious.

DIXON. You go to a rave? Is that it? Like in some big warehouse with drugs?

BERNARD. No. I thought Julie already told you that we were at –

DIXON. Wesleyan? Come on, I'm not an idiot. I know my own kid better than that.

I'm just so goddamn curious! You know? We give her no boundaries, no restrictions, so what the hell could she be so embarrassed about? Is this about sex, is that it?

BERNARD. No.

DIXON. With…either gender.

BERNARD. Mr. –

DIXON. It's Dixon, please.

BERNARD. She wasn't doing anything wrong, Dixon, I promise.

DIXON. Sex isn't wrong. Sex is good. Sex is beautiful.

BERNARD. This isn't about sex.

DIXON. Did someone get hurt? Is she in trouble?

BERNARD. No. It's nothing, really.

DIXON. And yet. The mind speculates. The infinite permutations.

Especially now. With my health. You know. The whole prostate thing.

(*Pause.* **DIXON** *leans in.*)

You'll understand this a lot better when you're older, Bernard. Especially when you're a parent. But there's nothing scarier than the unknown. As long as you can put a face to it, put a name to the thing you're up against, then no matter how bad it is, no matter how ugly or uncomfortable or even illegal, then at least you know. But *not* knowing. That's the worst. That's the shit that keeps you up at night.

(*silence*)

BERNARD. If I tell you where we are – just where we were – will you swear not to tell Julie?

DIXON. Of course.

BERNARD. Just so you stop worrying.

DIXON. I understand.

BERNARD. Just the location. That's it.

DIXON. Cross my heart.

BERNARD. Only because, I don't think Julie gets a sense of how these things affect people.

DIXON. No, I don't think she does.

(*silence*)

BERNARD. Last weekend. I don't know why she's making such a big deal out of it. But. Uh. My church had a retreat to New Jersey. So. I brought Julie along. That's it. Teaneck, New Jersey. That's where we were.

(*more silence*)

DIXON. Did you say *church?*

BERNARD. Yeah.

DIXON. But. Julie's Jewish.

BERNARD. Agnostic, actually.

DIXON. And are you… Christian?

BERNARD. My family belongs to New Light Korean Baptist in Queens. Me, I mostly just go on all the free trips.

DIXON. Huh.

(*beat*)

Huh.

BERNARD. I'm going to go get the poster.

(**BERNARD** *exits to* **JULIE***'s room.*)

(**DIXON** *sits with the information.*)

(*After a while,* **BERNARD** *returns with the poster.*)

Please don't tell Julie.

DIXON. Just one question. Was it ironic? Her going to church.

BERNARD. I promised I'd tell you where we went. That's it.

DIXON. Right.

BERNARD. Thanks for the weed.

DIXON. (*distracted*) Yup.

(**BERNARD** *exits.*)

Huh.

5.

(Dinner that night. **DIXON** *unpacks Chinese food containers from a take-out bag.* **JULIE** *enters in her practice clothes. She goes straight to the fridge. Grabs a bottle of Gatorade and takes a sporty gulp.)*

DIXON. Jesus, you're a beast.

JULIE. I get really thirsty.

DIXON. I see that. *(She burps.)* How did your presentation go?

JULIE. What presentation?

DIXON. Didn't you have some presentation this week?
I remember you saying something yesterday about it.

JULIE. *(on guard)* Yeah. It was fine. We got an A minus.

DIXON. Hey. Way to go.

JULIE. Why didn't you make dinner?

DIXON. I was working, lost track of time.

> *(***JULIE*** takes another chug of Gatorade.)*

You know Jules, you can talk to me. We're buds, right? We go way back.

JULIE. Like, to my birth?

DIXON. I'm just saying. If there's something you want to talk about.
Anything on your mind –

> *(The door opens.* **PAM** *returns from work. She puts down her bags, laptop, etc.)*

PAM. Chinese? I thought you were gonna cook?

DIXON. Yeah, my MSG count was down, so I figured…

PAM. How was practice?

> *(***JULIE*** doesn't respond.)*

Ah. I get the silent treatment. You lie to *me*, but I'm the one who's punished.

(JULIE *digs into the Chinese food bag. She dumps an* *entire container of rice onto her plate, carbo-loading.*)

DIXON. *(to* PAM*)* How was your day?

PAM. Fine. Frustrating. Fine.

DIXON. Any drama in the land of Documentary Programming?

PAM. No – this guy pitched a thing on Mormon cave dwellers, but I think the market's over-saturated with Mormon stories.

Did you get a lot done today?

DIXON. Slow but steady.

PAM. Oh! One of my co-workers. Her husband works in publishing, so I gave her your email. I figured why not, right?

JULIE. I'm getting a fork.

(PAM *hands* JULIE *a fork.*)

PAM. You know what I was thinking, Jules. Maybe we could go to a museum or something this weekend. You don't even have to talk to me. We can just watch the art silently together.

JULIE. I have practice.

PAM. On a weekend?

JULIE. Yeah. We've got championships coming up.

PAM. What about brunch Sunday morning. Before practice. We could all go.

DIXON. I never turn down a good brunch.

JULIE. Sunday morning…uh. I can't. I've got plans.

PAM. What plans?

JULIE. I have something with Bernard.

PAM. Well. He can come too. I'd love to meet him.

JULIE. Sorry. We have stuff to do.

PAM. Can you be more specific?

JULIE. No.

PAM. Why not?

JULIE. It's private.

PAM. You're sixteen. What private appointments could your schedule possibly contain?

DIXON. Ladies...

PAM. What? I'm her *mother*. I birthed her. She should be required to spend time with me.

DIXON. I'm sure she has a legitimate excuse. Right Jules?

JULIE. Yeah...

DIXON. And I'm sure, whatever it is, she's doing it responsibly and with caution, not letting herself get carried away or co-opted by whatever or whoever she's choosing to expose herself to.

PAM. Why are you talking like that?

DIXON. No, I just. We need to trust Julie, right? That she's making smart decisions for herself.

(They eat. Silence.)

Mormons.

PAM. Don't even get me started.

DIXON. You know what you should commission? A documentary on foreskins.

(JULIE *laughs. She finds her dad hilarious.)*

Like, what happens to them after they're – *(he gestures snipping)*

PAM. Okay here's the thing that drives me nuts about Mormons. Not the sacramental underwear. Not the everyone-gets-their-own planet thing. Not even that black people are denied Priesthood positions, because let's face it, there's racism and sexism in almost every religion. Not even the fact that they Baptized Jews who died in the Holocaust. What pisses me off is that even *after* numerous archeologists and historians and geneticists have *proven* that it is impossible for the "lost tribes of Israel" to have you know, showed up in America before the Native Americans and then be visited by Jesus Christ himself, even after all of this scholarship comes out, they still claim this as their origin story. Instead of saying, look, Joseph Smith was a fabulist. He was a scamster. We realize this story doesn't really make any sense – but we like it, so we're gonna keep perpetuating it and passing it down to our children. It's like you have to park your critical intelligence ten blocks away just to walk in the door.

(beat)

JULIE. How come you're always so condescending towards religious people?

PAM. How am I condescending?

JULIE. Like they all have Downs Syndrome or something.

DIXON. She never said anyone had Downs Syndrome. She was just making a point.

JULIE. But you think so. You think they're less smart.

PAM. Who?

JULIE. People of faith.

PAM. I didn't say that. Did I say that?

DIXON. No.

JULIE. You just said Mormons have no critical intelligence.

PAM. First of all, Mormons are their own class of crazy. Second, okay, yes, I will admit that I think people of "faith" have a less evolved worldview, I will cop to that.

JULIE. Why?

PAM. Why what?

JULIE. Why are they less evolved?

PAM. I didn't say "they" were less evolved. I said their "worldview" was less evolved.

JULIE. Why is their "worldview" less evolved?

DIXON. I think you're both speaking in extreme language right now.

PAM. It's fine. I can answer her calmly.

I think a religious worldview is less evolved because. And this is just my opinion. But I think religion was created by man at a time when he needed comfort, and now that we've outgrown it, it's *creepy* how many people are still clinging to the darkness instead of learning to ground their lives and value systems in the present tense.

JULIE. Creepy.

PAM. Also, the religious right is currently destroying this country.

DIXON. Okay, new topic!

PAM. They are! They've reached a level of fanaticism that is like... Fundamentalist.

JULIE. You're a Fundamentalist.

PAM. Excuse me???

JULIE. You're a crazy militant person. You're just as bad.

PAM. As....fundamentalists?

JULIE. As scary religious people.

PAM. I'm a fundamentalist...because I choose not believe in a collective delusion?

JULIE. You're a fundamentalist because you think you're right and everyone else is wrong.

PAM. When did I say that? When did I say everyone else is wrong?

JULIE. I feel bad for you.

PAM. What did you just say?

JULIE. At least religious people – they actually *care* about something. You don't care about anything. You just make fun of everything. And spew hate everywhere.

DIXON. Hey! Enough.

(*beat*)

PAM. Why would you say something like that to me?

(**JULIE** *shrugs, a little sheepish.*)

That is a very hurtful thing to say.

JULIE. (*quietly*)
Sorry.

(*Everyone sits in a sort of stunned, confused paralysis.*)

PAM. Wow. Okay.

DIXON. Pam –

PAM. No. It's fine. My daughter thinks I'm a hateful human being. It's very –

Is there any, um, lo mein left?

6.

(Pin-spot on **BERNARD**. *He clutches his battered copy of For Keeps.)*

BERNARD. Dear Pauline.

I'm sending this letter to your publisher at 375 Hudson Street. I hope it reaches you. I don't mean to intrude on your privacy, but I don't really know who else to ask. See, I'm having problems with this one shot. It's a POV shot, you know, subjective shot from the point of view of the main character, that acts as Julie, that's the main character, walking down Seventh Avenue. Kind of like in Agnes Varda's "Cleo from 5 to 7".

So my first question is: Is that lame? That convention.

Um. My second question is: Do you think a single camera shot has an entire history bound up in it? Like – will people see that shot and think, *oh, Agnes Varda.* Or will they see an insanely long tracking shot and automatically think, *oh, Orson Welles.*

I can't stop thinking in terms of all these titans of cinema and how the rest of us are ever supposed to break away from them.

Because I want to become a master artist too. I want to create something nobody's ever seen before. Something completely new and challenging and difficult and authentic. But... I don't know exactly how to do that.

How do you come up with a truly new form when all the tools you're using are from the past? How can you be both aware of the entire history of the thing you're making and not aware? How come that guy in *The Seagull,* directed by Sidney Lumet, goes out looking for new forms, gives up, and then kills himself?

(pause)

Hope you're doing okay up in Massachusetts. Can't wait to meet you in person one day. Your friend. Bernard Chang.

7.

(Continuous. A church pew. **BERNARD** *and* **JULIE** *kneel.)*

JULIE. Amen.

    *(***JULIE*** *opens her eyes.* **BERNARD** *gets his camera out.)*

    I like cathedrals.

BERNARD. Wait til this weekend. When there's incense and smoke and people.

JULIE. It's so quiet in here. Makes you think about things you don't normally think about.

BERNARD. Why don't you want to be Jewish?

JULIE. I'm still Jewish. Half-Jewish.

BERNARD. Okay. But why Jesus?

    I mean, why not Buddha. Or Xenu the intergalactic warlord.

JULIE. You think I'm making a mistake?

BERNARD. I think it's your choice.

JULIE. I choose Christianity.

    Pastor Bill? I like him. I like what he says about compassion. And grace.

BERNARD. Look – I'm not trying to talk you out of this. I just think you might want to figure out the whole Jesus thing before you get too far into it, that's all.

    (pause)

JULIE. What about you? Do you believe in him?

BERNARD. Yeah… I believe in Jesus. Not as much as my parents do. They probably have more pictures of Jesus than of me. But like, he's cool. He was the world's first pacifist, so I respect that. He was also a bad ass. Undermined authority. Hung out with lepers.

    *(***JULIE*** *closes her eyes again.* **BERNARD** *begins filming.)*

    Can you be a little more…animated?

JULIE. I'm praying.

BERNARD. There's no audio.

JULIE. So, bigger?

BERNARD. Remember that exercise we did on the retreat?

JULIE. Yeah.

BERNARD. Maybe you could try that?

(**JULIE** *stands on one leg and puts her hands together.*)

JULIE. "Do unto others as you would do unto yourself."
"Do unto others as you would do unto yourself."
"Do unto others as you would do unto yourself."
"Do unto others as you would do unto yourself."

(**BERNARD** *films.*)

More?

BERNARD. Keep going.

JULIE. "Do unto others as you would do unto yourself."
"Do unto others as you would do unto yourself."
"Do unto others as you would do unto yourself."
"Do unto others as you would do unto yourself."
"Do unto others as you would do unto yourself."
"Do unto others as you would do unto yourself."

(**JULIE** *starts swaying with the chant.*)

"Do unto others as you would do unto yourself."
"Do unto others as you would do unto yourself."
"Do unto others…"

(*She puts her foot down.*)

I need to sit.

(**BERNARD** *lowers his camera.*)

BERNARD. That's gonna look sick in black and white.

JULIE. I feel dizzy.

BERNARD. Did you feel something? Did you experience transcendence?

(*With real intensity. From her gut:*)

JULIE. Do you think I'm a freak?

BERNARD. What?

JULIE. Do you?

BERNARD. Yeah. But so am I.

JULIE. Really. Like that something's wrong with me.

BERNARD. Like what?

JULIE. Like…that I don't feel things.

BERNARD. You feel things. You feel things all the time.

JULIE. Sometimes I think I'm dead inside. Like, I'm just muscles and a body.

BERNARD. What? Hey. No. Come on. You're awesome.

JULIE. Just now. I didn't feel anything. I was saying the words, doing the exercise, but –

BERNARD. It doesn't always work like that.

JULIE. And then. Like, sex. Everyone is so *obsessed* with it. But I don't even think about that stuff. I don't even care.

BERNARD. Sex is overrated.

Look at me. I've only fingered one person. That's it. And it didn't even work. She was like. Uh, you have to move it around.

(**JULIE** *smiles.*)

Seriously.

JULIE. Who?

BERNARD. Sydney Kim. On last year's church bowling outing.

(*They both laugh at this.*)

Maybe you're a lesbian.

JULIE. What?

You wear a lot of sport bras.

JULIE. I'm not attracted to girls.

BERNARD. Yeah, probably not then.

JULIE. I wish I was a lesbian. Then at least I'd know I wasn't this retarded…robot person.

(*pause*)

BERNARD. You know who you should talk to about all this stuff?

JULIE. Who?

BERNARD. Your Dad.

JULIE. What?

BERNARD. He's really smart. I bet he'd have some good advice.

JULIE. When did you talk to my Dad?

Was he there!? When you went to my house?

BERNARD. Yeah. But – we only hung out for like ten minutes. Smoked a bowl.

JULIE. This is horrifying.

BERNARD. I just think if you're looking for someone to talk to.

JULIE. About?

BERNARD. Everything. Sex. Life. God.

JULIE. My parents don't believe in God.

BERNARD. Still.

JULIE. They don't believe in anything. That's the whole reason I'm here in the first place, remember?

BERNARD. I forgot.

JULIE. They think religion is stupid and that all religious people have mental problems, trust me. They wouldn't understand.

(pause)

Wait. Did you tell him anything? About last weekend?

BERNARD. No.

JULIE. Bernard. We're in a church.

8.

*(The apartment. Middle of the night. **DIXON** drags a sleepy **JULIE** into the living room.)*

JULIE. What are you doing?

DIXON. Shhh…

JULIE. I have a game tomorrow.

DIXON. Then I'll make it quick.

JULIE. It's like two in the morning!

DIXON. I know.

   Okay?

   I know.

JULIE. Know…what?

   (He gives her a look.)

   Bernard told you.

DIXON. To his credit, I had to pull out all the stops to get it out of him.

JULIE. Does Mom know?

DIXON. No. I haven't told her.

JULIE. She's gonna be pissed.

DIXON. She is not going to be pissed.

JULIE. Are we talking about the same person?

DIXON. I can handle her, okay?

   And for the record, I think you don't give her enough credit.

   She's trying her best.

   Everything she does is in your best interest.

   So. Cool it with the bitchy teenage attitude crap. Okay?

JULIE. Can I go now?

DIXON. No. We're gonna talk.

JUILE. … About?

DIXON. Well. I've been thinking a lot about Nietzsche lately.

JULIE. Seriously?!

DIXON. Entertain me. He was a smart guy, Nietzsche.

JULIE. I know who Nietzsche is.

DIXON. He said: given the premise that God is dead – human beings have two choices of how to go on living in that absence. We can either feel extremely anxious-you know, like little sailboats on a vast horizon-less ocean. Or, we can dance on the edge of a great abyss.

JULIE. God isn't dead.

DIXON. Just. In this example. It's a thought-experiment. Otherwise, you following?

JULIE. Yes. But I disagree with the premise.

DIXON. That's fine.

JULIE. So… Given your dumb premise. Which one does Nietzsche recommend?

DIXON. I don't know about you, but I pick dancing any day over being stuck on a sailboat.

JULIE. Aren't they the same thing?

DIXON. No. They're opposites. The boat scenario evokes being sad and trapped. The dancing, basking in enormous freedom.

JULIE. They sound the same to me.

DIXON. No. They're different. How do you not see this?

(pause)

JULIE. I'd rather be a ship then.

DIXON. No one *chooses* to be the ship.

JULIE. I do.

DIXON. No you don't.

JULIE. Uh huh.

DIXON. Why do you want to be a ship?

JULIE. Because. The abyss sounds lonely.

DIXON. It's not lonely. It's fun. That's why there's dancing.

JULIE. I'd still rather be a boat.

DIXON. Everyone's already in the boat…it's a given… maybe I didn't explain it right…it's not really an either or…it's a…it's both…never mind.

You get the point though, right? You get what I'm saying?

JULIE. No. I'm going back to bed.

DIXON. Wait! Wait! Wait! Wait!

This author I like. He says this thing: "You get to choose what to worship." Pretty neat, right?

(beat)

JULIE. Okay.

DIXON. Let me ask you something. If you could be anything when you grow up. Anything in the world. What would it be?

JULIE. A basketball player.

DIXON. Come on.

JULIE. A basketball player. For the WNBA.

DIXON. You want to wear mesh shorts as an adult?

JULIE. It's just a uniform.

DIXON. Fine. Say you end up playing for the WNBA. You're the Malcolm Gladwell of women's basketball.

Now, people worship different things. Some people worship money. Some people worship God. Some people worship themselves. Celebrities worship themselves. You, in this example, would worship basketball. See my point?

JULIE. I don't worship basketball.

DIXON. Hypothetically. That would be your chosen altar.

JULIE. Dad. It's two in the morning. What are you trying to say?

DIXON. Good question. What I'm trying to say is – We all worship things. Me, your Mom. We worship things too. Everybody worships things. Meaning. It's all relative.

JULIE. What is?

DIXON. The things we worship.

I just want to highlight the fact that you have complete and absolute freedom on this planet. All doors are open to you. Your horizon is limitless.

Which means. That while all these amazing doors are open to you – the minute you walk through one of them, the minute you choose one over another, you close off other potentially exciting door options.

Like. You know. Just for example. Maybe you'd like to learn German.

JULIE. I hate German.

DIXON. Well, okay, that's a little extremist.

JULIE. You don't want me to be a basketball player?

DIXON. Sure, if you want.

JULIE. You don't think I'm good enough?

DIXON. I think you're very good. You're very talented. I was just using basketball as an example.

JULIE. You haven't even seen me play.

DIXON. I've seen you play.

JULIE. Not lately. Not since I've gotten good.

DIXON. I had a tough year. Personally. You know that.

JULIE. I'm first-team all-Ivy.

DIXON. And I am very proud.

JULIE. It's sad you don't believe in me.

DIXON. Hey. I believe in you.

JULIE. Then why do you want me to learn German?

DIXON. I don't. That was merely to illustrate, you know, metaphorically, your freedom of –

The choices we make are important. Christianity, that's a choice. That's all I'm saying. Think carefully about the choices you make.

(beat)

JULIE. You smoked weed with Bernard.

DIXON. …I offered it to him. He accepted.

JULIE. He's my friend. Not yours.

DIXON. I was trying to be a good host.

*(**JULIE** stands.)*

Where are you going? You don't want to keep talking?

JULIE. Not really.

> (**JULIE** *starts to go. Turns around.*)

You've changed. You used to be different.

DIXON. How?

JULIE. I used to worship you. Now you don't even leave the
house.

> (**JULIE** *leaves* **DIXON** *alone in the dark.*)

9.

(Pin-spot on **BERNARD**.*)*

BERNARD. Hey Pauline. It's me. Again.

How's it going. I hope you're not too cold up there in Massachusetts. Maybe you're curled up on the couch watching an old movie. Radiator hissing. Snow, like a big white ocean, right outside your window. Maybe you have a dog. I picture you with a dog for some reason. Something fierce, but gentle. Like a spaniel. Or a wolfhound.

Wow. I realize I know absolutely nothing about you – except for that book jacket photo which is probably from like 1992.

Do you ever feel small? Sitting up there in your wood cabin? I've been feeling smaller than usual lately. I guess everybody does. Do they? You don't have to answer that.

I was reading through some of your old reviews last night. You write with so much clarity. It's like the whole world is flashing by in strobe light and you can see right through everything, right through to the real, concrete stuff. I really admire that. That…certainty. And you. Have I said that before? I admire you a lot. A lot a lot.

Best wishes, Bernard.

10.

(Continuous. The Apartment. **PAM** *holds a pamphlet in her hands.* **DIXON** *stands caught between her and* **BERNARD**.*)*

PAM. *(reading)*
8am: Pancake Breakfast.
10am: On Fire For the Lord!
11am: Woodworking.

DIXON. I didn't tell her, Bernard. I swear.

PAM. I found this pamphlet in Julie's room. In her desk.

DIXON. See? She found it. On her own.

PAM. It's for a religious retreat.

BERNARD. Is Julie coming?

PAM. She's…on her way.

BERNARD. So then. When she texted me…?

PAM. She left her phone here. I was just borrowing it.
It was a desperate move, I know that.

BERNARD. Just to um, clarify. Julie has no idea that you texted me from her phone?

PAM. We'll tell her as soon as she comes home. I will take this hit. Not you.

BERNARD. Maybe I should just come back later?

DIXON. Look, you're not in trouble here Bernard.

BERNARD. I'm not?

DIXON. No. You're caught in the middle.

PAM. I'm just trying to understand. Julie doesn't talk to me. She has shut me out. And I know that you went with her, on the retreat.

*(***BERNARD*** *looks to* ***DIXON***.)*

BERNARD. Dude!

DIXON. I had to tell her once she asked.
It's different with married people. There's a porous boundary.

PAM. Julie was raised atheist, you realize.

DIXON. I'm Jewish, Pam's lapsed.

PAM. I am not lapsed.

DIXON. Pam's nothing.

PAM. I'm secular. My parents were Marxist professors. Sorry, can we go back to the beginning? You and Julie went to…

BERNARD. There was a free trip organized by the Youth Group I belong to.

PAM. And you're…

DIXON. Christian.

BERNARD. Baptist. My family belongs to New Light Church in Flushing.

PAM. Why?

BERNARD. Why what?

PAM. Why did she go? Was she curious?

BERNARD. I don't know.

PAM. Was it her first time?

BERNARD. Yes. I mean. Well. No. Um.

PAM. So this is bigger, then?

BERNARD. No. What I mean is: She came to church with me a few times, but this was her first retreat.

PAM. And what happens on a retreat?

BERNARD. It's…mostly talking. And hanging out.

PAM. Is there Bible Study? More religious kind of stuff?

DIXON. *(to PAM)* You read the schedule. They did woodworking. Ate pancakes.

PAM. Obviously there's more to it than that.

DIXON. So we'll ask Julie. Right? We don't need Bernard. Let's send Bernard home. We'll talk to Julie over dinner.

PAM. Yeah, like Julie's gonna tell me the truth about anything.

(*back to* **BERNARD**) Bernard. I just have a few more questions. Does Julie believe in *God?*

BERNARD. I…don't know.

PAM. Has she converted? Has she made any kind of formal commitment?

BERNARD. I really don't feel comfortable talking about this with you…

PAM. I just want to know what we're dealing with here. What we're up against.

BERNARD. Maybe…you should talk to Julie then? Cause. You know. She's the one…

(*pause*)

I don't mean to be rude. I respect you guys both a lot.

PAM. Of course.

(**PAM** *turns away. Silence.*)

DIXON. Do you want water? I think we forgot to offer you something when you came in.

BERNARD. Yes, please.

DIXON. I'm on it. I will get you that water. Water for Bernard. Coming right up. (**DIXON** *gets him a glass of water.*) Want beer? We've got beer too.

BERNARD. What?

DIXON. Kidding. Just water. Very democratic choice. Very age-appropriate.

(**DIXON** *hands him the glass.*)

BERNARD. Thanks.

(**BERNARD** *downs the whole glass in one gulp.*)

DIXON. Want more?

BERNARD. Yes please.

(**DIXON** *refills the glass.* **BERNARD** *drinks.*)

PAM. Why didn't you say anything?

DIXON. I thought I could handle it.

PAM. So. You waited?

DIXON. I made a pact.

PAM. With Julie?

DIXON. No. With Bernard.

PAM. …What?

DIXON. Not like a formal treaty, but yeah. We had an understanding.

BERNARD. He said he had prostate cancer.

DIXON. Enlarged. I said enlarged.

PAM. So did you or did you not talk to Julie about this?

DIXON. I tried – I think my approach was a bit too philosophical, but…I was waiting for you. So we could form a united front.

PAM. You were waiting for me to…

DIXON. …find out.

PAM. How was I supposed to find out if no one told me?

DIXON. You're a highly perceptive person. You're very… perceptive. Come on. I told you. I waited. But I told you.

PAM. I can't even look at you right now.

DIXON. C'mon, I've handled this pretty diplomatically…

PAM. Our daughter might be *brainwashing* herself and you thought it was diplomatic to not say anything?

DIXON. At least I didn't jeopardize Julie's one and only friendship by impersonating her –

PAM. What else was I supposed to do!?!? NO ONE'S TALKING TO ME IN THIS HOUSE!

DIXON. Okay, okay. I'm here for you. I am on your side.

PAM. I feel so alone right now. I've never felt this alone before. How could you think this wouldn't upset me? How could you think I wouldn't be upset?

(*Enter* JULIE. *They look at her.*)

JULIE. What's…going on?

(*beat*)

BERNARD. They texted me.

(Off **PAM***'s reaction,* **DIXON** *stops talking.)*

PAM. Julie. I know it sounds crazy. What I did. But – you have to understand. No one's talking to me. And then, I found this in your room. *(She holds up the pamphlet.)* And I asked your Dad and *he* said he had this conversation last week with Bernard. So – I just wanted to hear it for myself. That's all.

*(***JULIE** *takes this in.)*

JULIE. You went through my stuff?

PAM. I was going to do your laundry for you. Which, expanded into a slightly larger, um.

JULIE. Okay. So. You know. I'm a member of New Light.

PAM. When you say…"member."

JULIE. Of the congregation.

PAM. Okay. Okay. I'm not mad. I think you think I'm going to be mad, but I'm not.

JULIE. *(quietly)* Okay.

PAM. Unless you're doing this as some sort of rebellion against me –

JULIE. Oh my god!

PAM. Right. This isn't about me. I think the next step is to sit down and discuss this as a family.

JULIE. Why? So you can talk me out of it?

PAM. So we can make a decision *together.*

JULIE. Its not your decision to make. It's my decision.

PAM. Well. I'm sorry, but you're too young to make this kind of decision on your own.

DIXON. Julie – tell Mom about the little boat. About Neitzsche.

JULIE. No.

DIXON. She just needs to be reassured –

JULIE. It doesn't matter. It's too late.

PAM. Too late for what?

JULIE. I love Jesus now and he loves me.

PAM. Sorry?

JULIE. Judge not, that ye be not judged. Matthew seven one.

(beat)

PAM. Go to your room!

JULIE. What? Why...?

PAM. Because... You're grounded.

JULIE. For talking?

PAM. For... I don't know. It doesn't matter. I need time to think.

JULIE. Dad – am I grounded?

DIXON. No, you're not grounded. We don't ground in this house.

PAM. Dixon!

DIXON. We don't ground! I'm not grounding anyone. I'm sorry.

PAM. Right.

Of course.

(beat)

Bernard – it was so nice meeting you.

*(**PAM** exits. Silence.)*

JULIE. Come on, let's go shoot stuff for your movie.

BERNARD. Are you sure? Are you okay?

JULIE. I'm fine. I just want to go work on your film.

DIXON. The black-and-white thing?

JULIE. It's really good. He's going to send it to Pauline Kael.

DIXON. Pauline Kael?

BERNARD. Yeah.

JULIE. She's a famous film critic.

DIXON. *(offhand)* Isn't Pauline Kael dead?

BERNARD. What?

DIXON. Isn't she? Pam would know.

BERNARD. She's dead?

DIXON. Some disease, maybe Parkinson's. A few year's back. Sorry – did someone tell you she was still alive?

BERNARD. No.

DIXON. Great critic. Kind of a bitch sometimes. But great prose style. Sharp wit.

(BERNARD *can barely stand.*)

I should…check on Pam.

(DIXON *exits.*)

(JULIE *approaches* BERNARD.)

JULIE. You okay?

BERNARD. I'm such an idiot.

JULIE. You're not an idiot.

BERNARD. What kind of idiot doesn't know –
Doesn't look up –

(*silence*)

JULIE. Hey. Let's pray.

(*She takes* BERNARD*'s hand as they kneel for Pauline Kael.*)

Dear Lord, Please help Bernard through this time of loss. Please show us your compassion and mercy as he tries to get through this time of pain.

(PAM *and* DIXON *re-enter. They watch as* JULIE *and* BERNARD *pray for Pauline Kael.*)

End of Act One

ACT TWO

1.

*(Later that night. **PAM** sits alone reading the Bible, highlighter in hand. After a while, **DIXON** enters.)*

DIXON. Whatcha reading?

PAM. King James, by way of Gideon International.

DIXON. We own the Bible?

PAM. I think we stole it once from a hotel.

DIXON. Ah yes, our thieving outlaw days.

PAM. Want?

*(**PAM** reaches into **DIXON**'s weed stash and pulls out a joint. She lights it, takes a deep inhale, extends it to **DIXON**. He stares at the joint, knowing the full implication of the question.)*

DIXON. I'm allowed to smoke, right? Cause you're smoking.

PAM. Like you actually give a shit.

*(**DIXON** takes the joint.)*

Julie's not in her room.

DIXON. I let her go out to pizza with Bernard.

PAM. Of course you did.

*(**DIXON** inhales.)*

This house. There's so much sneaking. Everyone's sneaking around.

*(**DIXON** exhales.)*

DIXON. So is he any good? Gideon.

PAM. I thought there would be more violence and "thou shalt not" and *we hate gay people* but its more "And this person said to that person, who met with this person, who conferred with that person..."

DIXON. Sounds like law school.

PAM. I keep reading. Looking for whatever Julie sees in this.

DIXON. Read me something.

(**PAM** *flips through the book and finds a passage.*)

PAM. "Tribulation worketh patience; And patience, experience; and experience, hope." That's Paul.

DIXON. That's actually kind of sweet, when you think about it.

PAM. Is it? To me it just sounds like a Hallmark card.

DIXON. Read something else.

PAM. "I urge you brothers, in the name of our Lord Jesus Christ, that all of you agree in what you say, and that there be no divisions among you, but that you be united in the same mind and in the same purpose. For it has been reported to me about you, my brothers, by Chloe's people, that there are rivalries among you." (*She looks up.*) Chloe? Who's Chloe?

DIXON. Maybe she's a rebel leader. Or, a prostitute.

PAM. I have failed my child. She's turning to *Chloe* before turning to me. We need to sit her down. Talk her out of it.

DIXON. I'm not doing that.

PAM. So this is fine with you.

DIXON. It's not ideal, but I'm not gonna scream at her about it.

PAM. She can't do this. She can't just *become* a Christian.

DIXON. She's not *becoming* anything. She's curious. And what's *so* terrible about Christianity? From my perspective, it means she'll be abstaining from sex, and maybe spend time volunteering at a soup kitchen.

PAM. I don't want Julie thinking she was born a sinner. She was born at Columbia Presbyterian.

(beat)

We should have raised her Jewish.

DIXON. She is Jewish.

PAM. She's half. And only culturally. But maybe if we had made a stronger push. Given her more structure.

DIXON. There's tons of creepy stuff in Judaism. For the record.

PAM. At least it's about questioning things. Not, superstition.

DIXON. *(with a Yiddish accent)* And what's so bad about a little superstition?

PAM. Oh come on. Believing in angels. Or that you'll crawl out of your own grave one day and be resurrected. It's such bullshit. *(a sudden, horrible thought:)* What if she's pro-life?

DIXON. Then we'll disown her.

PAM. I'm so nervous right now. I feel like I've been cracked in half.

DIXON. How about some Boggle? I'll crack open a bottle of wine –

PAM. Do I look like I want to play Boggle right now?

DIXON. We could go a movie. We haven't gone out in a while.

PAM. The world isn't one giant amusement, Dixon.

DIXON. I know that.

PAM. No, you don't.

DIXON. I get it. You're upset. Message received.

PAM. It's like you and Julie are the kids and I'm the adult.

DIXON. Woah.

PAM. You know, I see the way you two look at each other sometimes. Like you're conspiring.

DIXON. So *I'm* getting in trouble now?

PAM. And then the way you look at me. Like I'm Ursula the Sea Witch. Like I'm a big, fat purple Joan Collins,

ruining everybody's fun. You think I like being the
responsible one?

DIXON. Is this about the Bernard thing? Is that what this is
about?

PAM. No. But your choice there was very indicative.

DIXON. What choice?

PAM. Siding with him.

DIXON. Oh come on, I did not *side* with him.

PAM. You did. Actually. Which is wrong on so many levels.

DIXON. I fucked up. Okay? I got high. Got a little too
friendly with Bernard. I should have told you
afterwards, but I didn't because I didn't want you to
know that I missed my shift at that stupid Food Co-op.
Can we please move on!?

(*beat*)

PAM. You got high with Bernard?

DIXON. Not high. The kid took like two puffs.

PAM. Sorry. I'm just – You smoked weed with a teenager?

DIXON. To loosen him up. He wouldn't have talked
otherwise, trust me.

(**PAM** *stands up.*)

PAM. Oh my god.

DIXON. He barely touched it.

PAM. Oh my god!

DIXON. He was curious about it. And I provided him a safe
space to try it. Better me than some sleezy Senior at a
house party.

PAM. How do you not see how inappropriate that is?

DIXON. Well, I guess we all have our blind-spots.

PAM. What is that supposed to mean?

DIXON. Nothing.

PAM. No? Say it. Finish what you started.

DIXON. Pam. I love you. You're the smartest, sexiest woman I know. But. You're a bigot. You have become... bigoted.

PAM. Um.

DIXON. You're at like Chistopher Hitchens level of extreme dismissal of people of faith.

PAM. I'm...not.

DIXON. You are.

PAM. I'm...secular. I have strong secular beliefs.

DIXON. You're a bigot.

PAM. Stop saying that. That's an ugly word.

DIXON. Yeah, well. It's not the most beautiful personality trait...

   (beat)

PAM. Wow.

DIXON. Whatever, it's not like I'm a shining specimen of human behavior. I'm a snob. I smoke way too much weed. I clearly have boundary issues.

   (PAM stands up and walks over to a bookshelf.)

   C'mon – Pam. Pammy. I'm sorry. Okay? I shouldn't have called you that word. That was cruel of me. That was an exaggeration.

   (PAM picks a book off a shelf.)

   What are you doing?

   (PAM flips to a certain page. DIXON realizes what book she's holding.)

   I don't think you should do what you're about to do.

PAM. *(reading*)* "First case is Schneiter versus Magruder," Spicer announced as if a major antitrust trial was about to start.

   "Schneiter's not here," Beech said."

---

* Dixon's following two lines of dialogue, denoted by quotation marks, is a passage from John Grisham's *The Brethren*.

"Where is he?"

"Infirmary. Gallstones again."

(*silence*)

Should I keep going?

DIXON. I think you made your point.

PAM. I figured – I should read some John Grisham. See where the bar is. I started with "The Firm" a few weeks ago. Then "The Runaway Jury." About the tobacco industry. Which was pretty good. Then. "The Brethren." And I was reading it on the subway, on my way to work yesterday, and... When I came to this passage. I stopped breathing. I couldn't breath.

(*silence*)

So. Is there a book? Or are you just, retyping –

DIXON. There's a book.

PAM. So you just retyped passages of John Grisham...for fun?

DIXON. No. I did that so I would have something to read you. When you asked.

PAM. I don't understand.

DIXON. You wanted me to write a legal thriller. So. One document on my computer is a legal thriller. And then there's another document, in a folder labeled "Vacation Photos," which is the book I'm actually writing.

PAM. So then. What's the book you're actually writing?

DIXON. Please don't.

PAM. What?

DIXON. It's...embarrassing.

PAM. If you're too embarrassed to tell your own wife, then why are you writing it?

(*beat*)

DIXON. It's uh, about a man who is having an affair with the daughter of a French diplomat.

PAM. 'Kay.

DIXON. The man. He's just suffered a nervous breakdown and he's living as an expat farmer in Provence. And at the Saturday market, he meets this woman. This beautiful, carefree woman who turns out to be the daughter of France's ambassador to the United States. And they start up this affair. And it gets rather... pornographic.

PAM. How old is the daughter?

DIXON. Young. Julie's age. Maybe a little younger.

(This sinks in. Maybe a few tears trickle down **PAM***'s face.)*

PAM. So. While you're fucking me, you're actually fucking an imaginary French teenager?

DIXON. You make it sound like I'm cheating on you.

PAM. Aren't you?

DIXON. No. No.

(silence)

It's just a book. I can throw it away. I'll stop writing it. Look – I'm deleting it from my computer right now. Done. Deleted. Say something. Please. I've been fearing this moment for a long time and I need you to say something.

(beat)

PAM. *(quietly)* You don't even go to her games.

DIXON. What does that...?

PAM. Me, I have an excuse. I work long hours. But I would. I would be at every one of Julie's games if I could. It's not like you're busy. You're sitting home smoking pot and writing pornos.

DIXON. Why do you think that is? Huh? It's humiliating. All those fathers. Bankers. Doctors. Wall Street –

Oh look. Isn't that the guy who had a mental... Who used to be some hot-shot attorney but now...

And for you to even say that. For you to even suggest…
That because I skipped a few of her high school
basketball games, Julie is a spiritual nomad. I am very
kick-ass father thank you very much! And for you to
question that? For you to… You think I care if she
wants to be a Christian? She can join the goddamn
Tabernacle gospel choir if she wants. Stamp a burning
cross onto her forehead. Whatever she wants. I support
her. I don't judge. I'm not judging.

PAM. You think…I judge her?

DIXON. Why do you think she felt the need to lie about
this? You think that's an accident.

PAM. I don't judge her.

DIXON. Fine. I didn't say anything. You're a Saint. This is
all my fault, clearly. You're fucking Mother Theresa
and I'm a worthless deadbeat. That's why Julie always
comes to me instead of you.

2.

*(**BERNARD** stands in a pin-spot.)*

BERNARD. Hi, Pauline.

(He can't think of anything to say. Lights.)

3.

(**JULIE** *and* **BERNARD** *at the laundromat.*)

JULIE. My parents were fighting again last night.

BERNARD. I'm sorry.

JULIE. They think I can't hear. They keep going into the bathroom.

BERNARD. My parents are fighting too.

JULIE. Why?

BERNARD. I told them I wanna apply to film school. They want me to apply to MIT, like every other Asian on the planet. Maybe I should just go to MIT. My film sucks anyway.

JULIE. What are you talking about? It's great.

BERNARD. It doesn't make any sense.

JULIE. So?

BERNARD. I'm a fraud. I read all this shit about movies and talk about movies and fantasize about movies but then I don't know how to actually make a movie.

(*beat*)

JULIE. Hey. You know all those close-ups of my face?

BERNARD. Yeah.

JULIE. Do you think you could cut some of them?

BERNARD. Why?

JULIE. I don't like how I look. Up close.

BERNARD. You have great bone structure. And your face catches the light well.

JULIE. Just, some of them. The extreme close-ups.

BERNARD. I'll look at it.

(*beat*)

JULIE. Could you. Do you think you could kiss me?

BERNARD. Like, now?

JULIE. There's no one here, just homeless lady. Just so I know what it feels like.

BERNARD. Um.

JULIE. You don't have to finger me or anything.

(*beat*)

BERNARD. Sorry. I just. I don't think it's a good idea.

JULIE. Why not?

BERNARD. Because.

JULIE. Are you gay?

BERNARD. What!?

JULIE. People at school think you're gay.

BERNARD. Whatever. People at school suck.

JULIE. I'm just, letting you know. As your friend.

(*silence*)

BERNARD. Fine. I'll do it.

JULIE. Yeah?

BERNARD. Yeah.

(**BERNARD** *leans over and kisses* **JULIE**. *While he's kissing her, she takes his hand and places it on her chest, over the shirt. She holds his hand on her boob.*)

JULIE. Was that – normal?

BERNARD. Sure.

JULIE. I don't see what the whole big deal is.

4.

(Sunday morning. **JULIE** *sits in the living room in a prayer position. Maybe she wears a t-shirt that says "God Recycles.")*

*(***PAM*** *enters. She looks awful. Her hair is stringy, her face sleep-deprived. She waits for* **JULIE** *to finish praying.)*

JULIE. Amen.

PAM. Why aren't you at Church? Isn't Sunday morning services?

JULIE. Bernard's busy. So. I figured I'd just pray at home.

(beat)

PAM. You know Jules.

I've been thinking a lot. And. I wanted to say. In hindsight, I realize my initial reaction to your decision might have been a bit…and I hate this word, but… bigoted. I have been majorly closed-minded about this thing that you're curious about and that was just sucky of me.

JULIE. Okay.

PAM. Really?

JULIE. Yes. I accept your apology.

PAM. That is…very big of you.

JULIE. I'm still pissed at you for going through my things, for texting my best friend pretending to be me –

PAM. Okay –

JULIE. But. Jesus would want me to accept your apology, so. I do.

PAM. Well, thank goodness for Jesus then, right?

(beat)

How come Dad gets a free pass?

JULIE. He doesn't.

PAM. He does. You've been terrorizing me for months. You don't even look me in the eyes anymore. But Dad – Dad's the best. Dad's spotless.

JULIE. I dunno. It's just easier with him.

(silence)

PAM. I've been reading this blog by an Episcopalian pastor. Which I know is not the same thing as Baptist. But he's from Brooklyn. And he's really cool. Really smart. He talks a lot about community. Line being a part of something. And I know you don't really have a strong community at school…

JULIE. It's not about community.

PAM. Fine, not community. Acceptance. Belonging.

JULIE. No.

PAM. So tell me. Tell me what you're attracted to. Why Church?

JULIE. I…can't. Explain it.

PAM. Yes you can. You're very articulate when you want to be.

JULIE. It's not something you can just explain. With words.

PAM. Church is a building, let's start with that.

JULIE. It's not a building. It's more…like a family.

PAM. Okay. That's… Keep going.

JULIE. Like, for example. Last week. I did this thing called an altar call. It's where you go up on stage and everyone puts their hands on you so you can receive the Holy Spirit. And then afterwards there's all this hugging and some people are crying.

PAM. And did you receive it? The Holy Spirit.

JULIE. A little. I felt something in my shoulders. Just for a few seconds.

PAM. And when you say *felt* –

JULIE. Ugh.

PAM. I'm just trying to be as precise here as possible.

JULIE. So you can make fun of it?

PAM. No. No.

JULIE. This isn't helping.

PAM. Well, it's helping me and your decision affects both of us.

JULIE. I don't know what you want me to say. I like church. It makes sense to me.

PAM. What about God?

Can you describe him? Or her?

JULIE. It's not a person.

PAM. So then, it's more of an idea. A concept.

JULIE. It's more of a…relationship.

PAM. With?

JULIE. Like… To the world.

PAM. Okay… That's interesting. I never thought of that. Huh.

JULIE. It's like…in Calculus. You know Infinity?

PAM. Yes. It's an imaginary number.

JULIE. So this whole idea of dividing things by zero. It doesn't make any sense, right? Like – you can't even comprehend it. It hurts your brain just to think about it. What is zero? And what does it mean to divide a number by it since numbers are also these crazy incomprehensible abstractions? That's like Jesus. You agree to believe in him, even though he isn't really there.

(pause)

PAM. You're brilliant. Do you know that?

JULIE. No.

PAM. You are so goddamn smart.

(beat)

JULIE. Do you believe in heaven?

PAM. No.

You want me to be honest, right? I think when you die, you die. Maybe parts of you float around the universe or end up in the soil, but no. I don't believe in heaven.

JULIE. Do you love Dad?

PAM. What?

JULIE. Unconditionally. Like the way God loves people.

PAM. Why would you even ask me that.

JULIE. How come you two have been fighting so much lately?

PAM. We're just. We're going through something right now.

JULIE. You think he's a bad writer.

You think his book is going to suck, that's why you don't love him anymore.

PAM. It's...more complicated than that.

JULIE. I believe in him. If you loved Dad, you'd believe in him too. And support him no matter what he's going through.

PAM. Alright. That's enough.

JULIE. I'm just saying. You wouldn't have doubts. You'd just believe.

PAM. I believe.

JULIE. No. Not really. Not like – with your whole being.

PAM. Look Julie. Love – It's not black and white. Okay? It's more complicated than that. It's –

(pause)

You know. I don't see what this has to do with religion.

5.

(Pin-spot on **BERNARD***)*

BERNARD. Dear Pauline.

I'm writing to let you know there's a typo on page 473 of your book. It's not a huge mistake but, someone should probably do something about it. Also. Why did you call *Return of the Jedi* a quote "junkie piece of moviemaking?" I actually like that movie. It has flying motorcycles! And it's not like you ever made a movie. You're just a critic. You've probably never even held a camera. So. Yeah.

Best. Bernard.

6.

(The bleachers of a high school gymnasium. Loud basketball sounds. **DIXON** *sits alone, highly uncomfortable, clutching a book. He tries to watch, but can't totally follow. Maybe sometimes he even opens the book and reads.)*

(People start clapping. **DIXON** *takes a cue from the crowd and tentatively claps along.)*

(He feels weird. Maybe he goes back to his book. Maybe he fiddles with his glasses.)

(The crowd starts clapping again. **DIXON** *joins in.)*

DIXON. Okay. Why are we clapping? Oh. Now we're not clapping. Done with that.

(He forces himself to suck it up and watch. Over time, he forgets the other fathers, forgets his self-awareness and gets sucked in. He focuses on **JULIE**. *Finally,* **JULIE** *gets the ball.)*

… Jules. Pass it. Throw the thing…

(He watches.)

She's open. The girl with the thighs. With the spandex. C'mon… She's open – look at her.

(Maybe he stands.)

JULES! Throw it! Pass!

*(***JULIE*** passes. They score.)*

YES! Fucking. Yeah!

(To an unseen crowd member.)

No, you watch your language, Bill Blass. That's my fucking kid out there!

7.

(Up on the roof. **JULIE** *and* **BERNARD** *stare into a baby pool.* **JULIE** *wears a bathrobe over a bathing suit.)*

JULIE. I wrote down some questions. Can I read them?

BERNARD. Sure. It's your ceremony.

JULIE. My mom was asking me all these questions the other day and it got me thinking about stuff. So, I'll just read them.

*(***JULIE*** digs out a piece of paper from her robe.)*

(reading)

Question One: Why is the world so confusing?

Question Two: What makes people cruel to each other?

Question Three: Why is God still punishing people for sins they committed thousands of years ago?

Four: How come we can't cure cancer?

Five: Why are there so many homeless people in New York City?

Six: How do I *feel* God's love and not just know that it's there?

Seven: Is *feeling* different than *believing*?

Eight: Why do girls my age talk about sex and blowjobs all the time?

Nine: Why do we learn about things like gravity in AP Physics even though it doesn't exist but we don't learn about things like God.

Ten: Does the entire universe fit inside something else we can't see, like a fist?

Eleven: How come, when your brain decides to do something, like forgive someone, you can't always do it?

Twelve: Why do my mom and I not understand each other any more?

Thirteen: Why does just talking about religion fill so many people with hatred?

Fourteen: If the entire planet is going to explode or disappear one day, why do people care so much about things like being immortal?

Fifteen: Is being asexual a disease?

Sixteen: Why does my Dad smoke so much?

Seventeen: Why is my Mom falling apart?

Eighteen: Do things become clearer as you grow older or do you just get better at settling for smaller answers?

Nineteen...

Oh. That's it.

(*silence*)

BERNARD. You realize he doesn't actually answer you. Like, talk to people directly.

JULIE. I know.

(**JULIE** *takes off her robe.*)

JULIE. I'm ready.

BERNARD. If you're cold, we can go inside and use the bathtub. Sprinkle Poland Spring on your head.

JULIE. I like the roof. It's ceremonial.

BERNARD. Okay. So kneel down.

(**JULIE** *kneels in the water.*)

Now...before I say the whole "I baptize you in the name of the Father and the Son and the Holy Ghost" dip-your-head-in-the-water thing, you just have to say: I accept Jesus Christ, my Lord and Savior.

(**JULIE** *kneels frozen, paralyzed.*)

Or just: I accept you, Jesus. That's the point of the Baptism. Letting him into your heart. Filling yourself with *his* love.

JULIE. I accept the love of Jesus Christ, my Lord and Savior.

(**BERNARD,** *a bit surprised, plows on.*)

BERNARD. I now baptize you in the name of the Father and the Son and the Holy Ghost. By dipping your head in this water-filled plastic kiddie pool, you will wash away your sins and be re-born…

(**JULIE** *suddenly dunks her full head under water. She keeps it down there for a scary amount of time.*)

Julie! Julie! JULIE?

(**JULIE** *comes up for air.*)

Hey! You just need a tiny bit…

(**JULIE** *takes a deep breath and dunks her head again. Stays down for another bit.*)

JULIE! I love you.

(*She comes back up.*)

(**JULIE** *takes huge gulps of air.*)

(*She's done dunking herself now.*)

JULIE. Nothing happened.

BERNARD. What?

JULIE. Nothing…happened.

8.

(On the set of some HBO show at Kaufman Astoria studios.)

*(**PAM** sits off to the side in a director's chair. She wears a headset and watches a scene that takes place offstage.)*

*(**DIXON** enters. He hovers behind her until the camera cuts, a giant buzzer goes off and the red light goes on. Maybe we hear the giant studio air conditioning go on too. **PAM** removes her headset. **DIXON** approaches.)*

DIXON. I had to walk through three different soundstages to find you. Food's better on Stage F by the way.

PAM. What brings you to Queens?

DIXON. My wife. She's disappeared.

PAM. Maybe she's sick of fighting with you. Maybe she wants to be alone.

*(**DIXON** digs a piece of paper out of his pocket.)*

DIXON. I was digging through some old boxes, trying to find our wedding vows. But I don't think we kept them. I think I wrote mine on an airplane cocktail napkin. Anyway. I came up with some new ones.

(He looks at the paper, puts it back in his pocket.)

You know what. I'll just wing it.

I, Dixon, vow to you, Pam, that I will quit smoking weed. I, Dixon, vow to you, Pam, that I will never lie to you again about books that I may or may not be writing. Nor will I plagiarize famous authors. Uh. I vow to start cooking again.

PAM. Can we not do this here, please?

DIXON. Where else are we gonna do it?

PAM. At home.

DIXON. Really? Because by my calculations, you leave home before breakfast and don't come back until after midnight.

PAM. I'm busy. I'm working.

DIXON. Bullshit. This isn't even your show. And since when do documentaries shoot on soundstages?

PAM. I'm allowed to be here. People visit from the Network all the time. So, I'm visiting.

DIXON. Can I keep going with my vows? I may be a talentless hack of a writer, but I'm a pretty okay public orator.

I vow to give more money to homeless people. That's part of my be-a-better-person campaign. I vow to stop being such a meaningless waste of space and to get my shit together so I can make Pam proud of me once again. I vow —

PAM. I get the point.

DIXON. Do you?

PAM. You're sorry. You adore me.

DIXON. Pam — I'm sorry you're disappointed in me, but get over it. I've apologized. Now it's your turn to take a step forward.

(pause)

PAM. I don't know anything anymore.

DIXON. What?

PAM. I'm forty-six and I don't know anything.

DIXON. You're pretty damn smart.

PAM. No, I'm an idiot. I have no answers. I go around acting like I have answers, but I don't. I can't even raise a kid. Or… Talk. And you know what the worst part is? I look at Julie. And I am so…jealous.

DIXON. Pam —

PAM. What do I believe in? Nothing. What do you believe in? We believe in nothing.

DIXON. I believe in things.

PAM. What do you believe in?

DIXON. I believe in…uh, democracy. Education. I believe very strongly in education. Family. You.

PAM. C'mon.

DIXON. What? I believe in you. You are the closest thing I have to a religion. You are everything I have invested in on this planet. Why does that not register to you?

PAM. It does.

DIXON. Then why are you hiding from me? Why are you sitting alone in a darkened corner, disgusted by my sheer presence?

PAM. Do you fantasize about younger women?

DIXON. Who doesn't fantasize?

PAM. Just answer the question.

DIXON. Yes. I fantasize. I have a thing for French women. It's a recent development. I was watching a lot of French New Wave films during my breakdown. See? I'm not hiding anything from you.

PAM. Are you still attracted to me?

DIXON. Yes.

(*beat*)

Sometimes. Most of the time. Which I think is a pretty healthy place to be in.

PAM. It's like these floodgates opened. And all this *doubt* has crept into my life. All these questions that I never used to have.

(*beat*)

DIXON. Look. It's pretty simple. I like you. You like me. I've got problems. You've got problems. I'm your best friend. You're my best friend. I think everyone else is lame and stupid. You think everyone else is lame and stupid. It's really not that complicated. We've made it work for eighteen years, why all of a sudden does it have to change?

PAM. Because. I have believed in you for years. When you took a job at a kinda gross and morally dubious law firm – I believed in you. When you made partner – I believed in you. When you walked out in the middle of a negotiation, leaving behind your career – burnt out – I believed in you. When you said you wanted to take

on the injustice of the American legal system despite
having zero background in fiction writing – I believed
in you. So, maybe I've reached my tipping point. And
I have lost my belief in you and I don't know how to
get it back.

DIXON. Well. Try harder. It's not like you're the easiest
person to love. But somehow I figured out how to do
it.

PAM. I don't want to fight –

DIXON. Neither do I. I'm just saying. I figured out how
to love you despite your myriad flaws. So maybe you
could suck it up and extend me the same kindness.
And how weak is your faith in me that you falter at the
first sign of trouble? Show some goddam fortitude.

PAM. You lied to me. To my face.

DIXON. I did. And you know what? I'll probably do it again.
Why? Because I'm a human being. Because that's the
dumb shit that human beings do to each other.

PAM. Not to people you love.

DIXON. Yes, to people you love. Especially to people you
love.

PAM. I don't want to be with a liar.

DIXON. Do you want to end this? Split up? Is that what you
want?

PAM. No.

DIXON. Good.

PAM. Maybe.

DIXON. Maybe!?

PAM. I don't know! That's why I'm sitting here, trying to
think my way through this.

DIXON. Well make up your mind already.

PAM. I can't give you any answer right now.

DIXON. Jesus Christ, Pam.

PAM. I'm sorry. I'm being honest.

DIXON. I'm in Hell. I am in my own personal version of hell with you.

PAM. Yeah. Well, me too.

DIXON. You are not in Hell. I'm the one who's in Hell.

PAM. I'm in Hell. You don't think I'm in Hell?

DIXON. You're in Limbo. You're in fucking Purgatory.

PAM. I'm in Hell! Fighting with you is Hell. So, I'm in Hell.

DIXON. That is not Hell! *I* am in Hell –

PAM. I'm in Hell!

DIXON. I'm in Hell!

PAM. I'm in Hell!

DIXON. I'm in Hell!

PAM. I'm in –

    BUZZZZZZZ.

(The Red Light comes back on and we're filming...)

11.

(Pin-spot on **BERNARD**.*)*

BERNARD. Hi Pauline.

How are things? How's…death?

Why am I even talking to you.

I finished my movie. I don't really know what to do with it now. I was going to send it to you.

Maybe I'll send it to some festivals. I don't know.

I got into a fight with my parents today. It's weird – we're complete strangers. *You* probably understand me more than my parents ever will.

Is that normal? To feel a connection with someone you've never met in person? Does that make it any less real?

You don't have to answer that.

I don't have a title for my movie. I was thinking of calling it: "Infinity." Or, "Oblivion." Or "Death and the Existential Void With Regards To Losing Your Artistic Hero."

Maybe… I'll check in with you tomorrow? If you're not too busy. I miss you.

I mean that. I miss you. Bernard.

12.

*(Continuous. The apartment has been re-arranged into
a make-shift movie theater. **BERNARD** has dressed up for
the occasion. He has set up an old Super 8 film projector
in the middle of the room.)*

DIXON. Where did you get an old projector?

BERNARD. The A.V. Club lent it to me. But we have to be
really careful because the motor belt broke last year.

*(**BERNARD** threads his film into the projector.)*

JULIE. Is she coming?

DIXON. She's on set.

JULIE. Why is she on set?

DIXON. I think she needs some alone time.

JULIE. I wanted her to see this.

DIXON. She'll see it. We'll do a second viewing.

BERNARD. Shit. Oh crap. Oh...shit. Shit shit shit shit shit.

DIXON. What?

BERNARD. The film – it just – ripped. See? It's really
delicate, cause it's old. It's my only copy.

DIXON. Can you glue it?

BERNARD. There's special tape – and this ruler – they have
it at school. I don't know how to – It's just gonna spool
onto the ground.

DIXON. I don't know Bernard. We might have to postpone.

*(Enter **PAM**.)*

*(**DIXON** freezes but tries to play it cool.)*

*(to **PAM**)*

Hey –

(He tries to catch her gaze, but she looks away.)

Bernard's film broke.

(She walks over to the projector.)

BERNARD. I don't have splicing tape.

> PAM *inspects the rip. She goes over and pulls out some scotch tape and, like second nature, tears off two tiny pieces and sticks them to both sides of the film. She clicks the projector on and off to see if it works. It does.)*

PAM. Tada.

> *(silence)*

So. What's this movie about?

JULIE. Me. And some other stuff.

> *(more silence)*

JULIE. I don't think I'm going to become a Christian.

DIXON. Why not? What happened?

JULIE. I just don't know if it's the right fit for me, that's all.

> *(Beat.* PAM *thinks for a moment.)*

PAM. Maybe. I dunno. Maybe don't give up so easily. You have to fight for the things you want.

> *(Beat.* JULIE *takes this in.)*

JULIE. Seriously?

PAM. Yeah.

> *(*DIXON *tries to make eye contact with* PAM. PAM *continues to avoid him.)*

DIXON. I agree.

BERNARD. Can we turn off the lights?

DIXON. Go ahead.

JULIE. I'll do it.

> *(*JULIE *gets the lights. Everyone takes their seats. They sit together, in shadow-y darkness.)*

BERNARD. So – this is my first film. Untitled. It's something that means a lot to me, so it's very special to get to share it with you guys instead of with my own boring uncultured immigrant family.

(**BERNARD** *gathers his thoughts.*)

First films are difficult to make, probably because you're doubting yourself the entire time. You lose your way a lot. But you have to start somewhere I guess, and this is where I'm starting. Oh. Also. This film is dedicated to Pauline Kael. Someone I never got to meet in person but who meant a great deal to me.

(**BERNARD** *turns on the film. Black and white shadows flicker on their faces and on the walls. He hits play on a boombox. Foreboding orchestral music floods the stage.*)

I added a soundtrack.

JULIE. It's terrifying.

BERNARD. I know.

(*The film plays.*)

(*Slowly, in the darkness,* **DIXON** *places his open palm out next to* **PAM**.)

(*His hand remains there like this for some time, dangling. The film continues,* **DIXON**'s *hand remains untouched.*)

(*The music and shadows continue.*)

(*Then – the music swells to a sharp strident note;*)

(*Everybody jumps.*)

(**PAM** *instinctively reaches her hand down, clasping* **DIXON**'s.)

(*They look at each other for a brief moment, desperate, pained, understanding.*)

(*They go back to watching the film.*)

(**PAM** *cries softly, her hand quivering in* **DIXON**'s *ever so slightly.*)

(*They continue holding hands, clutching each other in the darkness as the shadows grow larger and larger.*)

End of Play